PERKY PELICAN

HAPPY READING!

This book is especially for:

_____

Suzanne Tate
Author—
brings fun and
facts to us in her
Nature Series.

James Melvin
Illustrator—
brings joyous life
to Suzanne Tate's
characters.

Author Suzanne Tate
and
Illustrator James Melvin

PERKY PELICAN

A Tale of a Lively Bird

Suzanne Tate

Illustrated by James Melvin

Nags Head Art

To Frank

who loved sharing
his knowledge of nature
with young friends

Library of Congress Control Number 95-72699
ISBN 978-1-878405-13-5
ISBN 1-878405-13-6
Published by
Nags Head Art, Inc., P.O. Box 2149, Manteo, NC 27954
Copyright © 1996 by Nags Head Art, Inc.
Revised 2005

Perky Pelican was perky!
He was lively as could be.

Perky lived on Sandy Island
with many other pelicans.

HELPFUL HUMANS made Sandy Island.
When they dug a deep channel for boats to use,
they piled up sand.

The sand formed an island —
a safe place for Perky and his family.

Perky's mother made her nest on Sandy Island.
She placed sticks one at a time on a bush.
Then, she covered the sticks with grass.

Perky's mother laid two eggs in her nest.
And Perky's papa took turns with her
in caring for the eggs.

They kept the eggs warm by wrapping
their feet around them.
Mother Nature gave pelicans hot feet!

Perky was the first to hatch.
He pecked and pecked so hard —

that the egg nearly jumped out of the nest!

Perky's little sister, Pammy, hatched three days later.
She was smaller than he.

At first, Perky and his sister had no feathers.
They looked like baby dinosaurs!

"I wish we had feathers like you,"
Perky said to his mother.

"Don't worry. Your papa and I will take
care of you," his mother said.
"And soon you will be covered
with soft, white down."

The pelican parents also took turns
feeding the chicks.
They stuffed them with fishy food.

Soon Perky and Pammy were snow-white —
just as their mother had said.
And every time dinner flew in,
Perky was lively.
"Here I am, here I am!" he squawked.

Sometimes Perky stuck his whole head
in his mother's bill to grab food.
He was so hungry.

Perky and Pammy Pelican grew and grew.
Patches of brown feathers began to show
on their bodies.

Nine weeks went by, and Perky grew to be a large bird
with strong brown feathers.
He spread his wings and felt proud.
"Look at me now!" he squawked.

"Well, it's time for you to learn to fly
and catch your own fish," said Perky's papa.

Perky lifted up his wings and soon could fly
above the water around Sandy Island.

He watched some pelicans as they dived for fish.
The big birds dropped from the sky head first.
Splash! Then, they scooped up fish in their big beaks.

"That looks easy," Perky said to himself.

Straight down he came. Splash!
But he didn't get any fish!
Perky knew he had to keep trying.
He dived again and again that day.

At last, he began to catch a fish or two.
A little gull came and sat on his head —
looking for a free meal!
"This kind of fishing is for the birds.
There must be an easier way to fish," thought Perky.

He watched a long line of pelicans
flap their wings and glide.

"I'll follow them," Perky said to himself.
His big wings lifted him into the air.

Soon, Perky saw a FISHERMAN and his boat.
He was taking "fatbacks" out of his net
and throwing them to pelicans.
(HUMANS don't like to eat fatbacks, but pelicans do.)

Perky flew down and landed on the water.
The FISHERMAN threw him a fatback.
Perky grabbed it right away.
And that fish was gone in one gulp
down Perky's gullet!

A pretty little pelican swam up to Perky.
"I'll show you how to get lots of fish," she said.

Perky perked up his head.
Then, he saw that it was his little sister, Pammy!

But Perky noticed something
had happened to her.
"How have you been?" he asked politely.

"I hurt my wing one day when I was
diving for fish," she replied.
"Now I can't dive very well."

"But I've learned an easy way to fish,"
his sister said. "Come, let me show you."

Pammy swam beside the net,
pulling out fatbacks one by one.
Perky followed her, and he too tugged
from the net all the fish he wanted.

The FISHERMAN watched them.
"Thanks for helping me clean my net," he said.
"You can have your fill of fatbacks
anytime you wish."

The FISHERMAN started his motor
and headed for the dock.

The pelicans felt full and happy!
"Thanks for showing me an easy way to fish,"
Perky said to Pammy. "Let's look
for the FISHERMAN tomorrow."

Then, Perky Pelican — always a lively bird — led the way
home to Sandy Island.